For Elsie

This paperback edition first published in 2021 by Andersen Press Ltd.

First published in 2020 by Andersen Press Ltd.,

20 Vauxhall Bridge Road, London, SW1V 2SA, UK • Vijverlaan 48, 3062 HL Rotterdam, Nederland.

1 3 5 7 9 10 8 6 4 2

British Library Cataloguing in Publication Data available. ISBN 978 1 78344 951 4

ROBERT STARLING

FERGAL MEETS FERN

ANDERSEN PRESS

This is Fergal.

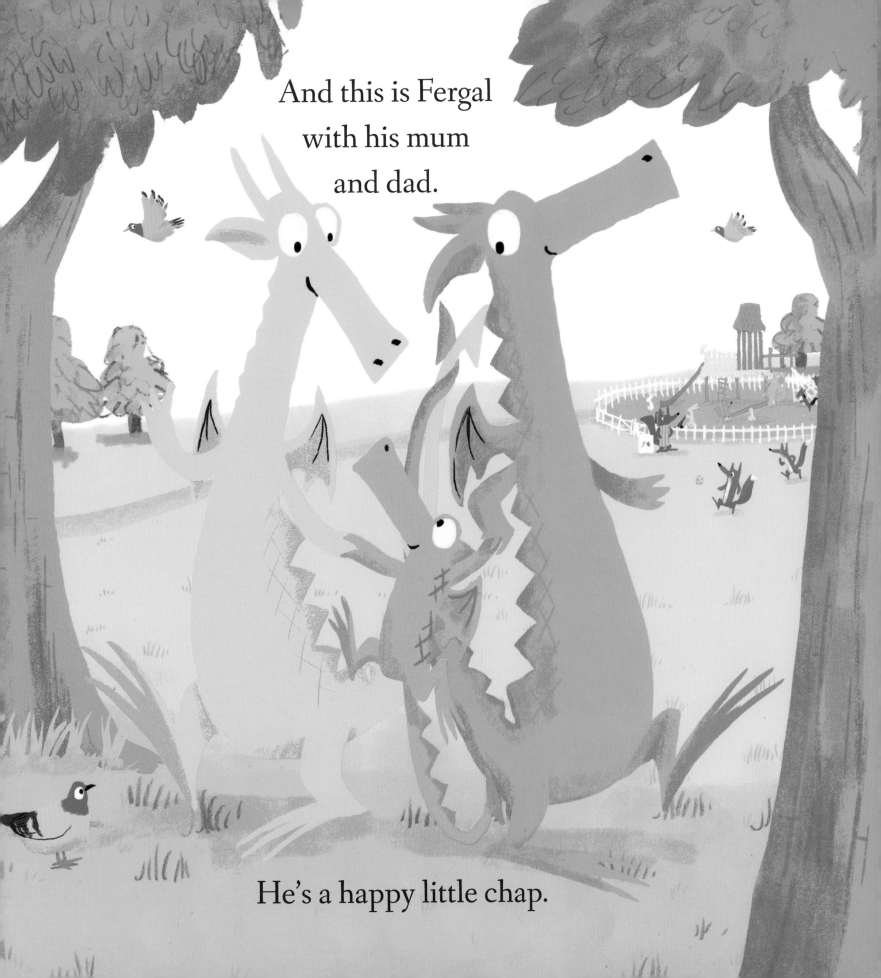

And this is Fergal
with his mum
and dad.

He's a happy little chap.

Or he was, until
Mum and Dad
brought home
the egg.

It didn't do much at first.

Everyone just watched it and waited.

And then one day, it hatched!

Inside the egg was Fergal's new baby sister, Fern.

Suddenly, the house was full of visitors coming to meet Fern and give her presents.

Fergal was starting to feel a bit funny until Nan-dragon brought a present for him too. Tickets for the flying show!

But Fergal's good mood didn't last long.
From bedtime to playtime Fern spoiled everything.

She played with his toys. It made Fergal feel **fiery**, but he kept it to himself.

She cried in the car. It made Fergal feel **really fiery**, but he kept it to himself.

WAAAAAA!

Then, on the day of
the flying show, Fern got sick.
"I'm sorry darling," said Mum,
"but Dad needs to get Fern's
medicine, so he can't take you
to the flying show.
We'll all go another time."

FLYING
display

As they went to
buy the medicine,
Fergal felt the fiery feeling building up inside him.

No one noticed him. No one ever noticed him. He decided to **run away**.

When Dad realised
Fergal had gone he
was really worried.

Everyone helped to look,

but no one
could spot him.

It was Dad who finally found Fergal.

"I was so worried," he said, wiping away Fergal's tears. "Why would you run away?" "I didn't think you'd care," gulped Fergal, "now you've got Fern."

"Why didn't you tell me how you were feeling?" asked Dad. "Let's get some fresh air."

Fergal told Dad that
sometimes Fern made
him feel fiery. He knew it
was wrong, so he kept the
feeling secret.

"Feelings aren't right or wrong," said Dad.
"But keep them bottled up inside and they can hurt you."

Fergal said he felt jealous because Fern got everyone's love. "Babies need a special kind of love, because they're so new and little," said Dad.

"It was the same when you were small. Take a look."

little artist

It was Fergal's baby book! Inside he could see Mum and Dad doing all those baby things with him.

ne Fergal!

Dinner time!

Asleep at last!

First steps!

Later, Fergal had another feeling to tell
Dad about: he felt worried because
everything was so different now.

"One big thing that is different is you, Fergal," said Dad.
"I'm not different!" said Fergal.

"Yes, you are," said Dad.
"You're a big brother now."

fugle!

Fergal thought about it.
He liked the sound of that.

Finally Fergal told Dad about feeling sad because everyone always looked at Fern.

"Have you ever noticed who Fern always looks at?" asked Dad. Fergal didn't know. "She looks at you, Fergal. When she does, what do you think she sees?"

Fergal thought. He was always fiery or worried or sad or jealous when Fern was around.

"I guess she sees... a grumpy big brother."

So Fergal decided to make a change.

And it turned out Mum and Dad were so busy,

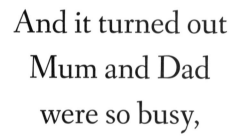

WOOOOOSH!!!

CLICK!

that a big brother had a really important job to do.

Something that would make
sure Fern remembered exactly
how Fergal felt about her.
Because...

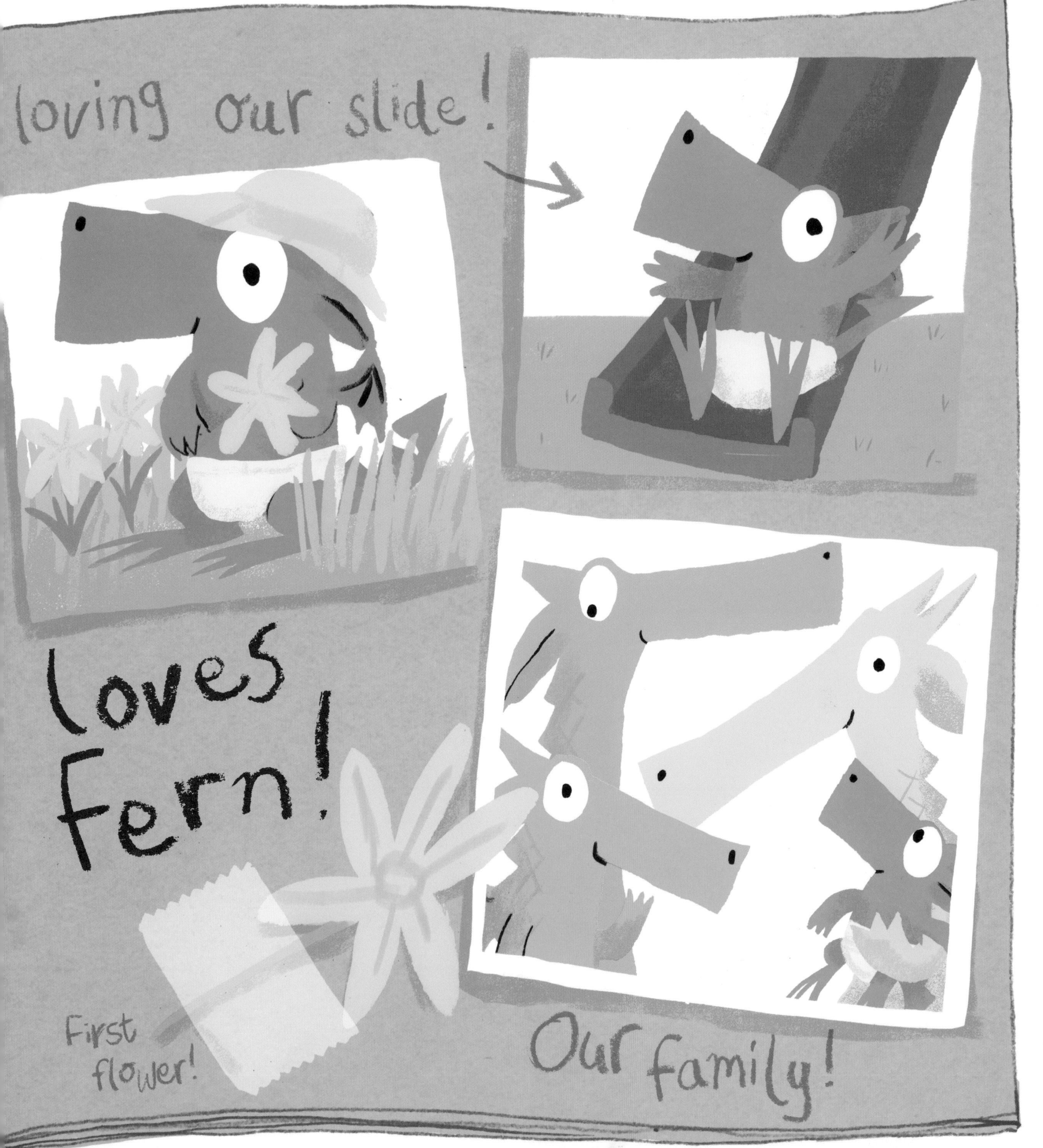
loving our slide!
loves Fern!
First flower!
Our family!